THE NAMELESS MAN

Also by E.E. Cooley

Prime Youth: Prisoners of The Masquerade

The Nameless Man

Copyright ©2022 by Ethan Cooley

ISBN: 979-8-9860413-4-6

Contact Info: www.eecooley.com

Cover design: Ethan Cooley

Editors: Karen Proofreads (karenproofreads.com), Pamela Greer (pageeditingservice.com)

Second Edition Paperback March 2024

To all of you who feel your "thing" will never go away. To all of you who are broken and feel like you will never be fixed. To all of you who feel no one should love you because of what you've done or what's happened to you. To all of you who just want it taken all away.

PROLOGUE

"Why should I bother living anymore?" That's the question I fell asleep to last night, and it's the same question I've asked myself for the last few months.

But I know I want to live. I have very fond days of my life that I cherish. I want more of those days. But I have many more days that I would rather forget. And those are the only days I remember. And those days seem to be the most recent days of my life.

The only positive I've had is my wife. I love my wife. I love her so much. And she loves me back. She's been there for me through this season of my life. Because it wasn't always like this. I never doubted my life or the purpose of living—that never happened. But one day while working my current job, something happened that I still can't describe to this day.

I was overcome with fear, but I didn't know what I was afraid of. I just knew I was afraid. Before this, I had been thinking about death, and my mind started spiraling from there, and next thing I knew, I was bawling out of fear into my wife's shoulder. Since then, I haven't been the same, and I don't know if I ever will be. But I know that as soon as I'm out of this job, the job that started all of this, everything will be back to normal.

Because now, my mind can start spiraling at any moment—normally, when I least expect it. And the fear from that builds and builds until it all comes out in a panic attack, for lack of a better term.

But this now affects my entire life. It impacts my sleep, my love life, the few relationships I have, my work, and every other facet of my life.

Like I was saying about the job, my job is about to end. When it ends, I'm scheduled to leave on a rocket that will take my wife and me to a spaceship that's ready to take all its passengers away from Earth to start a new life. Right now, Earth is in utter disarray. Water is becoming more and more scarce, riots and looting fill the streets, no one feels safe anymore, disease is rampant, overpopulation grows to be more of a concern by the hour, and food is as scarce as water.

My life is a mess, just like the world around me. But that will all change once this job ends and I'm among the stars.

PART 1

"Why do you want to leave the planet?" the interviewer asks.

"Why wouldn't I?" the man replies. "The world has gone to crap." The man blinks several times and gulps before continuing. "I can't find a job, my family is starving, and I just want to live knowing that there will be food on the table three times a day and a roof over our heads." The man blinks several times again.

"You can get whatever is in your eye, sir," the interviewer says.

"There's nothing in my eye."

"Then why are you blinking?"

The man gulps several times before replying. "I'm fine. Next question, please."

I write "Tourette's?" on my evaluation paper and bite the back of my pen.

"What do you have to offer to the other folks you'll travel with?" the interviewer asks.

"I'm good at fixing stuff."

"Have you ever worked on any of the gen three ships before?"

The man readjusts. "No. I work more with appliances and other household items." The man gulps again as he waits for the next question.

"That'll be all, sir. Thank you." The interviewer sticks his hand out and the two shake hands. The video dies shortly after, the projector turning off.

With the room left in darkness, I sit longer than I should, just staring at the empty wall. This job is crap. The same thing day after day. Nothing new. Nothing interesting. Just the same darn thing day after day.

I finally grab the remote on the table next to me and press the Blinds button. The giant window wall to my right starts to appear as the blinds are rolled up into the ceiling, letting in the now setting sun.

I thought this view would never get old, but unfortunately my disdain for my job has crept over into the other facets of my life.

I take the evaluation paper off of my board and roll up the paper, stuffing it back in the slot in the Video Cylinder, or Vidcyd, as I call it, next to the projector lens. Twisting the lid back into place, I feel the magnets catch and lock the lid in place. I take it off its stand and put it back in the delivery tube. With the door closed and sealed, I pull the floor holding the Vidcyd and watch it fall. I still don't understand how the Vidcyd is shot from the ground all the way up here.

And another boring day is over. I make my way to the sliding door behind me and enter the family room. Across the room is the open-concept kitchen. I grab two plates and silverware and set the table.

This is the only time of the day that I somewhat enjoy. Talking to my wife till I go to bed. Just talking till we can't talk anymore.

With the table set, I grab our two boxed meals and toss them in the warmer.

As I watch the boxes turn in circles, someone comes up behind me and wraps their arms over my shoulders. I grab my wife's hands as she sets her head on my left shoulder.

"How was your day?" she asks.

"Same as all the other days. Did you expect any different?" I lean my head against hers and close my eyes, enjoying her warm touch.

"Yes. I expected an elephant to smash through the roof and have a tea party with you. What was I thinking?"

We both laugh as the warmer beeps. My wife lets go, and I bring the food to the table. Tonight's meal is potato casserole with green beans. We hold each other's hand while we eat.

"So, who did you get today?" my wife asks.

I take another bite before answering. "I had a guy with Tourette's, another guy who lost an arm, and a widow with three kids. And the rest were all normal. Nothing special today. That is, except you." I squeeze my wife's hand, and she smiles back at me. "What about your day?"

"Boring, like always."

We eat our food in silence as the sun dips below the window line.

My wife finishes her food and leans back, still holding my hand. "What would you like to do tonight? We could watch that new movie they sent up."

"I didn't see it. What's it about?"

"I think some new sci-fi movie by that big director."

"That Dave guy?"

"I think so. It didn't jump out at me."

"Nothing ever does anymore." I grab our dishes and bring them to the kitchen. The boxes go in the trash cylinder next to the sink, and an orange flash lights up the cylinder as the trash is incinerated. I run the dishes under the water, dry them, and put them back on the shelf with the other dishes.

My wife still sits at the table, looking out the window at the dying light, but looks at me as I approach. "Let's watch that movie." I hold my hand out to her.

She grabs it and we slowly walk the seven steps to our bedroom. We change clothes, and she wraps herself in her blue blanket and snuggles against me. I hold her and start the movie.

"How likely are we to forget this movie?" I ask.

"If the last . . . however many we've seen . . . are any indication, I'd say we'll forget it by morning."

As we watch the movie, the same questions keep running through my mind. What's the point of this? What's the point of any of this? To work, do something with my wife that I'll probably forget in a couple hours, and do it all again the next day. What's the point?

I wake up the next morning with my wife gone. I'm unable to remember what we did last night. The blinds are closed, with hints of light coming through the fabric. I lie in bed, not wanting to get up.

The clock reads 7:30, and I don't get a Vidcyd till 9:00. So I just lie here, mulling over how much time I have left. As an analyst for all of the people wanting to leave the planet, I automatically get to leave the planet after everyone is interviewed. The only problem is that I haven't left yet, and I need to leave.

Sometime last week I was given a note saying that every last human had been scheduled for an interview. Which meant I would be done soon, and my wife and I would be happier, living a luxurious life with the other people leaving the planet, traveling the stars till we die.

But then, what after that? What about after we die? That question bounces around in my head, leading to other thoughts and questions that make me start to fear. I shove my face into my pillow and try to calm down. I can't control my breathing. Then, after what feels like an eternity, I finally calm down. I relax and flip back over. The clock reads 8:15.

I can't be late. I yank the covers off and walk the five steps to the bathroom door. After sliding it open, I turn the light on and look at myself in the sink mirror. My hair is a mess, and I look like—like not how I want to look.

I get in the shower and stand under the hot water, just staring at the floor, with my hands on the back of my neck. I stand under it so long that my head becomes numb to the water. I don't even realize water is hitting my head until I start getting cleaned up.

I get out and comb my hair, looking again at myself as I go from what I don't want to be to someone who will never be who I want to be.

Through two more sliding doors from the bathroom is the walk-in closet with clothes that are all different, but all feel the same. No matter the color, no matter the feel. They just cover my body.

I throw on some slippers and make my way to the kitchen. I start the hot water heater and look in the cabinet for my tea bags, only to find the same stinkin' flavor I've had for the past year.

I pull the box out and grab one of the bags. I stare at the box and lean against the counter for a moment before pounding the box with my fist. When I'm done, the box starts to take its original shape, but it will never be the same. I put it back in the cabinet and grab one of the two cups on the shelf above it.

A beep goes off from the water heater, and I pour the water into the cup. I take it with me to the projector room and wait in my chair for the Vidcyd to arrive.

The same tea, the same chair, the same view, the same job, day after day after day, and for what? Is it really worth it to go through this pain to get better?

The Vidcyd smacks the top of the tube and jolts me out of my brain. I push the floor of the tube in, and the Vidcyd drops on it. I take it, open the lid, and pull out the rolled-up evaluation paper. I lay the Vidcyd on the stand next to my chair and turn on the projector. The wall across from me lights up with the words "Interviewee #49590" in black text against a white background, not much different from the rest of the house.

I sit down and close the blinds. I attach the evaluation paper to my board and bite the back of my pen as I wait for the interview to begin.

A middle-aged man appears. He definitely would hit it off well with the ladies.

"Why do you want to leave the planet?" the interviewer asks.

"I need to protect my family. Everyone is slowly tearing themselves apart. This is not a place I can raise my children."

"At least you have children," I mumble.

"How old are your children?" the interviewer asks.

"How is that relevant? Don't you already know that?" the man replies.

"We want to make sure our information is accurate."

The man says nothing for a while and looks at the floor, then looks back up at the interviewer before replying, "Nine and twelve."

"What can the two of them offer to the other folks they travel with?"

"My kids?"

"Yes."

"They're kids. I don't know how much you expect them to do. They're just going to be kids."

"So, they have no skills to offer?"

"I never said that. But why does it matter? I thought what my wife and I could offer would be more of your concern."

"Everyone has a role to play. They can't just *be kids*. They have to be able to do something."

"What do you expect kids to do in space? They're gonna have fun because they aren't living in the hellhole the earth has turned into!" The man yells and throws his arms up.

"No need to yell, sir."

"You've basically told me that my kids won't be leaving because they can't do anything! How else do you expect me to respond?"

"Nothing's been decided yet, sir. But yelling won't help you."

The man gets up and runs out of the frame. Yelling ensues, and a moment later, the man is dragged back across the frame by two men.

I write down "anger management" on my paper. "I don't think he's getting on," I murmur as the next interview begins.

***

I shove the Vidcyd back into the tube and slam the door, staring as it falls down to the earth. And I start my evening routine again, doing the same exact thing as the night before.

As I wait for the food to warm up, I lean against the counter and hang my head with my eyes closed. My brain doesn't even know what to think when my wife wraps her arms around my stomach. I grin as I take my hand and rub it against hers.

"Another bad day?" she asks.

"Why do I even bother?"

"Because this guarantees us a spot off this planet."

The warmer beeps and I bring the food to the table.

We hold hands again while we eat.

"Tell me you had a better day than I did.?" I ask.

"Why don't we talk about something other than work? Like the movie we watched last night. How was it?"

"The movie? We watched a movie last night?"

"Yeah. It was . . . oh, what was it? I can't remember."

I let go of her hand, and she makes a face at me. I lean back in my chair as she gets up and brings her chair next to me.

"What about some dessert?" she asks. "We still have your favorite."

"I've had my favorite the last year that we've been up here," I bark at her. She pulls back, scared, and stares at me. As I'm about to apologize, she gets up and goes into the bedroom.

I slam my fist on the table and shove my food off. The plate clatters to the floor but doesn't break.

I pull my hair and lay my head on the table and scream. I then start slowly banging my head repeatedly onto the table. Not enough that it hurts—just enough that I feel it.

3

It takes me forever to get out of bed the next morning. I just lie there with my eyes closed and let my mind run. I start off thinking about my wife—how beautiful she is, how awesome she is. That turns into how upset and scared she was last night. How she didn't even look at me when I came to bed, even though I knew she was still awake. That turns into how I'm a terrible husband. That my wife will forever be upset. How I'm a horrible human being and my wife will never love me again. How no one will ever love me again.

I toss and turn in bed, unable to find any comfortable position. Why should I bother? It's not like I'm worth anything.

As I turn over toward the clock, it reads 8:55. Finally, a distraction. I force myself up out of bed and shove some clothes on, not bothering to get any tea this morning.

As I watch more interviews, I think of how worthless I am. How all these people are worth something. They want to go to space and get off this planet. They have families and people who care for them. I don't even know what I want. Even if I did, I know I don't have anyone to tell.

When the interviews end, I sit on the sunken couch in the floor across from the dinner table. I sit facing the wall as I watch the sun set. Maybe if I went blind from looking at the sun I would be worth something to someone. Someone would have to take care of me. But that would probably ruin my chances at getting a spot on a ship off this rock. I also wouldn't be able to look at my wife's beauty—I'd have to remember it.

And that's when this small bit of hope creeps through. It reminds me that all these problems will be gone when you leave. The uneasiness, the wild thoughts, the trouble falling asleep. Just make it through and you'll be free.

The next thing I know, my wife sits next to me. "Bad day?" she asks, wrapping her arms around my neck and laying her head on my shoulder.

I hold her hands and nod.

"You've made it through worse, you know."

"Every time feels like the worst." I squeeze her hands harder.

We sit there in silence, unmoving. Nothing to do, nothing to say. So my mind starts running again. My grip slowly tightens on my wife's hands, but she doesn't say a word.

"Quit thinking," she says.

"I have nothing else to do."

"Then think about me. Think about all the good times we've had. All the times we've made each other laugh. Think about that."

For a moment, I have a reprieve. I loosen my grip on my wife's hands and close my eyes, this time not afraid I'll spiral.

But for an instant, my mind starts to wander, and I'm spiraling again. I open my eyes and stand up.

"Why is this happening?" I pace back and forth in front of the couch. "Why is it so bad this time?"

"Was it one of the interviews today?" my wife asks.

"It's all the interviews!" I yell at her and stop pacing. "Every stinkin' one. Every single one of those people has dreams, aspirations, drive. They're able to get up and go to the interviews. I have to force myself out of bed just to watch the same kind of people over and over again."

"Keep thinking about when we leave and how much better it will be."

"All I can think about is how I want this gone now. Not later." I wrap my hands around the back of my neck and close my eyes.

A moment later, my wife hugs me and nestles her head on my chest. She rubs my back while I grab her and squeeze her. I squeeze her so hard I'm surprised she doesn't pop, but she doesn't say a word as she continues rubbing my back. I lay my head on her shoulder as I begin to cry. I try to stop it, but I can't. Everything comes out. I don't even know what I'm crying about, but it all comes out.

I sound like a baby as I choke out sounds that have no meaning. Yet my wife takes it all like it's her pain. Through my sobs, I even make out that she's crying too.

****

With our tears having long ago run dry and the sun having set, leaving the room in darkness, my wife slowly lifts her head and whispers, "Let's go to bed."

Still holding her, I lift my head and see nearly the entire right half of her shirt is wet. "Looks like I ruined your shirt."

"A small price to pay."

We grin at each other as I guide her back to the bedroom.

"Feeling better?" she asks.

"A little."

"That's better than none."

As she opens the door, I ask her, "Do you love me?"

She stops and turns toward me. "Of course I love you. What kind of a question is that?"

4

I fall asleep with no problems whatsoever. But when I wake up, I still lie in bed until just a few minutes before work starts. This time, though, I lie in bed relieved. Relieved that I got an entire night's sleep, relieved that I fell asleep without thinking of . . . anything, really.

When I look at myself in the mirror, my hair isn't a mess from trying to pull it out the night before. My face still looks the same, but I don't feel the same. I feel rejuvenated, excited to be up and going.

I take one of my quickest showers and get dressed in my favorite blue shirt. I pull my favorite tea flavor from the box in the cabinet and set it in my steaming water, once again enjoying its flavor as I make my way to the projector room.

As I walk in, a Vidcyd pops up. Closing the blinds, I get everything prepared and power on the projector.

I'm excited for today. I can't wait to see the applicants.

"Interviewee #49681" flashes across the wall.

"Why do you want to leave the planet?" the interviewer asks.

The woman looks at the ground and rubs her hands together before replying. "I just want to get off this stinkin' planet . . . I just want to get off it."

"Any particular reason?" the interviewer asks.

The lady shakes her head.

"Everyone wants to leave the planet, ma'am. If you can't give me a reason to leave, you'll be in the back of the line."

"I'm gonna kill myself," she blurts out. "I'm gonna kill myself if I have to spend another second on this godforsaken planet."

I write "suicide" on my paper.

"Do you hear me, whoever is watching this?" The lady looks directly at the camera. "If I don't leave, I'm going to kill myself."

"That's all, ma'am," the interviewer says.

The lady gets up and runs in front of the camera. "I'm gonna kill myself if I don't go! Do you hear me?" Two men grab her and pull her away. "You have to let me go!" The wall goes black.

At least I'm not the only one, I think, as the wall changes to "Interviewee #49682."

"Why do you want to leave the planet?" the interviewer asks.

The lady runs her hands over her long-sleeve shirt. "I want this to stop."

"Want what to stop?" the interviewer asks.

The lady pulls her sleeves further down her arms, grabbing the ends in her fist. "I just want it to stop."

"Can you tell me what it is you want to stop?" the interviewer asks.

The lady hesitates. "The pain." She rubs her arms again.

I write down on my paper, "self-harm?"

"Is there anything you can offer the other folks who you travel with?"

The lady shakes her head. "I'm just another body that wants off this planet." She stares at the floor and rubs her hands up and down her arms. "I'm good with a knife, though." She looks back up at the interviewer.

"That'll be all, ma'am. Thank you."

***

I end the day with interviewee #49725, a man who lost his arm in a riot. I doubt he would be in the front of the line, but who knows?

As the projector turns off, I immediately raise the blinds and shoot the Vidcyd back down.

While I wait for the food to get warmed up, I pull out a glass of sparkling juice and the two fancy glasses. I pour the glasses, and my wife comes up behind me and wraps her arms around me.

"I see someone's doing better."

I kiss her hands as I finish pouring the second glass.

"You know me too well," I reply.

***

After dinner, we sit on the sunken couches with our glasses of sparkling juice, my arm around my wife, who is curled up against me as we watch the sunset.

"It's beautiful, isn't it?" she asks.

I take a sip of my drink and look out at the orange-and-red clouds. "It sure is."

We sit there in silence, just staring at the sun's beauty. Not once today had my mind wandered any. Not once had I thought about my purpose or why I was living. I had simply lived today. But I was afraid I would spiral again if I kept thinking about it, so I tell my wife, "I want to apologize for how I've treated you the past few days. It wasn't right of me to do that."

My wife looks up at me. "I should probably apologize for how I acted. It was wrong of me to leave you and not help you."

"You have no reason to apologize—"

"I have every reason to apologize. It wasn't right to leave you in your time of crisis."

I just smile at her. "How in the world did I marry the nicest person on the planet?"

"Maybe you just got lucky." She sets her glass on the floor.

"A relationship can't be built on luck," I say, setting my glass next to hers.

"Then what is it built on?" she asks, wrapping her arms around my neck.

I do the same to her and reply, "Love." We kiss for the first time in a while, and it feels amazing.

After kissing, we stare into each other's eyes for a moment before I ask, "You don't think you could take tomorrow off, could you?"

"You know I can't do that."

"Please?"

She grins at me and leans back. "I can't take off tomorrow, but why don't we make tonight special?" She grabs my hand and leads me to the bedroom.

5

The next five days are the best in my life. I sleep perfectly and wake up without lying in bed forever. I enjoy working and don't feel worthless after watching everyone.

My wife and I continue having great evenings where we just talk about all the good times and our hopes for the future.

"What do you plan to do when you first arrive?" she asks me as we sit on the bed.

"I want to find a window and stare out at the stars while holding your hand." I grab her hand and kiss it. "And what do you plan to do?"

"Well, there are a lot of things I plan on doing. But whatever I do, I want to do it with you." She touches her finger to my chest.

I grab her hand with both of mine. "Anything specific you want to do with me?"

"Definitely some dinners together, with the most expensive wine they have."

"You like wine?" I ask, cocking my head.

"Yes. Did you not know that?" she asks, leaning back.

"I never took you for a wine drinker."

"Then what did you take me for?" She tries pulling her hand out of mine, but I pull her closer so we are nearly touching noses.

"I know you're an amazing kisser."

We kiss.

When we part, she asks, "Really. What did you take me for?"

I brush a loose strand of hair behind her ear and reply, "I took you to be very loving, kind, compassionate, and someone who, no matter what came their way, would have my back."

She grins at me and hugs me. I hug her back, and we sit there for a while. After what feels like forever, my wife says, "I love you."

"I love you too," I reply.

6

When I see "Interviewee #50000" pop up, I am ecstatic. This is the last interview to watch, and I will be done. After this, I will be on my way to space, with no more worries of a job that swings from great to horrendous.

"Why do you want to leave the planet?" the interviewer asks.

The man stares at the interviewer for a moment before replying. "I actually don't want to leave the planet."

"Why don't you want to leave the planet?"

"I don't believe God is done with Earth yet."

Oh great, not one of these people.

"The earth is being destroyed, sir. You do realize that—right?"

"We thought the world would be destroyed from the First World War, and we made it." The man starts counting on his fingers. "We thought the world would be destroyed by the Second World War, and we made it. We thought the world would be destroyed by the Great Depression, and we made it. We think the world will be destroyed now, but I think we'll make it through again. If anything, you'll have the same problems in space, and probably more that no one has thought of yet. You're choosing to not face the problem and just cope with the problem."

"You do realize that the earth's water supply is being eaten up?" asks the interviewer.

"You really still believe that?" The man grins. "You need to wake up."

"If you don't want to leave the planet, then that will be all, sir. Thank you."

I write down on my paper, "conspiracy theorist, crazy."

This time, instead of the wall going blank, it shows a man seated in a chair. "Congratulations. You've completed all of your interviews. This means you and your family are now eligible for the next flight to our spacecraft that's ready to take the next generation beyond the bounds of Earth. Later tonight, you'll be picked up and escorted to our launch pads. From there, you'll get on a rocket and be free from this earth. Thank you for your time and dedication in helping us choose the next generation."

The man disappears and the room goes silent. As I sit there, I slowly start to smile. I raise the blinds and walk over to the window. Clouds fill the sky, but I imagine them clear with stars shining above when I whisper to myself, "Finally."

***

"So, what's the big news?" my wife asks as she sits down at the table with me.

"I just finished the last interview today."

"Really?"

"I got a message at the end of them today saying we'll be leaving tonight for the launch pads."

"Ha-ha!" My wife claps and gets up and hugs me. "I'm so proud of you."

"I'm just glad I made it through."

She steps back but keeps her arms around my neck. "I knew you would."

"And now all those problems will be gone."

We kiss, when suddenly the glass wall shatters. We look up and see men wearing all black standing in our family room.

I pull my wife back into the kitchen and stand in front of her. "Who are you?" I ask.

"We're here to arrest you, sir," says one of the men walking toward me.

"Arrest me? For what?"

"For crimes against humanity, sir. For the death of thousands of innocents."

I stand there, dumbfounded, when my wife replies, "He would never hurt a soul."

"Exactly," I reply.

The man stops and almost looks confused. "So, you're admitting to your crime?"

"Admitting to my crime? Did you not hear her?" I point at my wife behind me.

"Hear who?" the man asks.

"My wife. Are you blind?"

"There's no one behind you."

I look behind me and squeeze my wife's hand. "She's right here." I point to her again. "What is this?"

Then I feel a hand on my shoulder.

"It's time to go," says another man, grabbing my wrist that's holding my wife's hand. I turn around and find my wife gone, nowhere to be seen.

I wriggle out of his grasp and scream, "What did you do to her?"

"There's no one else here," says the man who was behind me.

I rush at him, and the next thing I know I'm on the ground and the world is getting blurry until it goes dark.

PART 2

7

Everything comes back slowly. I can hear people talking but only catch bits and pieces. I'm lying down, but I don't know on what. I see different colors, but nothing is clear—just brown and gray splotches.

Then I understand more of the voices, but they don't make any sense.

"His trial will be today," says a man.

"He's in no condition to defend himself," says a woman. "Give him at least until tomorrow."

"You really want this murderer sitting among us for that long?" asks the man.

"He may be innocent," replies the woman. "We don't know."

"Good luck finding anyone else who believes like you."

A moment passes before the woman yells, "We can't give up our old ways and turn into savages like the rest of the world!"

All my senses come back to me in a moment. I'm lying on a dirt floor surrounded by rock. In front of me is a door made of metal bars, with no spaces big enough for me to get through. Past the door is a hallway with other doors like mine and a light coming from the right side of my door.

I stand up and stumble a bit, falling onto the rock wall and scraping my hands. I can't remember the last time I felt pain. Physical pain, that is. I've had plenty of pain to deal with in the past year.

I walk up to the door and try to open it, but it just rattles.

"Don't waste your energy." I look up and see a man looking at me through the door across from me. He's sitting against the rock wall.

I shake the door some more and try shoving it open, to no avail.

"Did you not believe me?" the man asks.

I don't answer and look around the room. It's nothing but rock walls and a dirt floor. When I look around, I find my clothes to be a complete mess, all covered in dirt and grime. It makes me sick, seeing all this dirtiness.

I walk back over to the door and ask the man, "Where are we?"

"So, he's not a mute," he chuckles to himself. "Best guess is somewhere we don't want to be."

"How did you get here?"

"I was eating dinner when these guys wearing all black broke through my window and took me. I was seven days away from being on the next shuttle to space."

"The same thing happened to me. You didn't evaluate the interviews, did you?"

The man stands up and leans against the door. "I did," he says slowly. He starts to say something but stops himself. Then a giant blast rumbles through the room, shaking everything.

"What was that?" I ask, looking around.

"You said you worked with the interviews, right?" the man asks when the rumbles die down.

"Yes," I reply.

"When were you scheduled to leave?"

"Whenever I was taken. I don't know how long ago that was."

The man steps back from the door and balls his fists before slamming them against the door.

"What's wrong?" I ask.

"You were brought here last night." He slumps against the wall and sits down. "Which means that was the rocket taking off. That was our ticket out of here. Now we'll never get off the planet."

It takes me a second to process what he said, and when it sinks in, it hits me like a brick. "No, no, no." I shake the door with all my strength. I make so much noise that someone yells at me to quiet down.

I push myself away from the door and pace around the room with my hair in my fists. "This isn't going to go away now," I mutter to myself. "I don't want to go back. I don't want to go back."

That's when my wife jumps into my mind. "My wife." I rush over to the door, yelling, "Where's my wife?"

"Your wife?" the man asks. "You were the only one that came in."

"No. She has to be here. They did something to her."

"How could you have a wife?" the man asks. They only took applicants who were single and not in a relationship.

"I have a wife!" I yell at him. "She was by my side the entire time!"

A guard walks up from my right, wearing a bandanna and carrying a knife. "If you don't quiet down, I'll kill you before your trial."

"What did you do to my wife?" I yell at the guard.

"Did you not hear a word I said?" The guard raises his knife and steps closer my door.

"You can't keep her from me!"

"Put the knife down." A guard with an eye patch walks up and grabs the knife out of the bandanna guard's hand. "Go." The eye-patch guard shoves the bandanna guard away.

When he's long gone, the eye-patch guard points the knife at me. "If you keep making noise, we'll move your trial up and you'll be dead before you know it."

"Trial? Trial for what?" I ask, gripping the bars harder.

"For the murders you've committed. Did you not know that's what you agreed to when you took your job?"

"I've not murdered anyone!" I scream and shake the door. "I need to get out of here."

The eye-patch guard waves to someone down the hallway, and two more guards walk up behind him, one of them the bandanna guard.

"Away from the door," the eye-patch guard says. "Let me out!"

The guards open the door and pull me off the door. Two of them hold me by the arms while the third ties a cloth around my mouth and shoves a bag over my head. Then my hands and feet are bound together by something. I'm spun around, and fall to the ground when I hear the door close and lock. I try to sit up, but my hands are bound behind me. I wriggle around but can't seem to sit up. I start to panic and begin thrashing, trying to sit up. When I finally do, I bonk my head against something and end up lying down again. My mind starts racing and then spiraling before I'm back where I was just a few days ago. Fear consumes me as I start thinking about never getting off the planet, never being free from this pain, how I'll die full of fear, with no reason why it's consuming me. I'll die never getting better. I'll die a mess of a person that no one loves because I'm so broken and could never fix myself.

Where will I go when I die? Will the afterlife continue to torment me like I'm tormented now? Is there even an afterlife?

With the fear overwhelming me, I let it all out. I start bawling uncontrollably, this time with no one to hold me, no one to comfort me. No one who loves me, no one I can hold till I fall asleep. Just the dirty ground. A ground that feels no emotion, a ground that will never know fear. A ground that isn't alive.

As my mind doesn't stop spiraling, I cry myself to sleep.

I wake up to the sound of my door being opened. Several feet shuffle around the room before I'm picked up, still tied up and with the bag on my head, and my legs are freed.

I'm walked out of the room, guided by two people roughly holding my arms. I can hear a group of voices getting louder as we walk, until I hear another door open, and the voices bombard me.

"Murderer."

"You should be ashamed of yourself."

"Kill him!"

"You worthless piece of trash."

"Wake up, you idiot."

These harsh comments continue as I'm walked across the room. I'm set in a chair, and my hands are tied to something in front of me. Then the bag on my head and cloth around my mouth are taken off, and the scene in front of me is one I haven't seen in a while.

I'm in another rock-walled room, this one ten times bigger than my previous room. There are at least a hundred people gathered behind a wooden fence. I sit not too far in front of the fence with my hands tied to a post in front of me. A man sits on a raised platform to my left and starts slamming a pole onto the platform. It takes some time, but eventually the room quiets down.

"Today, we have subject seven here for his crimes against the people of Earth. Will the prosecution share their evidence?"

A man steps in front of the raised platform from my right. "This man is part of what all of you know as the Repopulation Program. As an interview analyst, he willingly sent people to their deaths."

"I didn't kill anyone," I blurt out.

"Quiet!" The man with the pole slams it against his platform again.

"As I was saying," the other man continues, "anybody that's a part of the Repopulation Program is considered a domestic terrorist and shall receive the death penalty for their crimes against humanity."

"I didn't kill anyone!" I yell.

"Liar," someone yells from the crowd.

"Quiet!" The man with the pole slams it again. "Does the subject wish to defend himself?" he asks, looking at me.

My mind goes blank as I stare out at the crowd of people. They all stare at me like they want to personally kill me.

"Well?" the man with the pole asks.

"I didn't kill anyone, okay? I don't even know what the Repopulation Program is. I was just evaluating applicants."

"You knew the whole time!" someone yells.

"I didn't know!" I yell. "I thought I was helping choose the order of who got to leave the planet."

"You definitely helped choose," someone else yells, "by killing them."

"I didn't do that!" I yell, standing up. "I just did my job and lived with my—where's my wife?" I look at the man with the pole. "Where's my wife?"

Another man walks up to the man with the pole and whispers in his ear.

"I've been told you had no wife sir," the man with the pole says.

"Yes, I do!" I walk toward him and get tugged back by the rope.

"He's crazy and a murderer!" another person yells from the crowd. A chorus of agreements follows.

"Silence." The man with the pole slams it again and waits until the crowd quiets down. The room is silent as the man with the pole looks at me. After a while, he finally says, "Do I have anyone in favor of an insanity plea that would replace the death sentence with life in prison?"

I'm not crazy.

The room stays completely silent as one hand is raised from the right side of the room—a woman standing against the wall.

"All in favor of the death penalty?" the man with the pole asks.

The entire room is silent as everyone else raises their hand.

"It's decided, then. You shall be executed with the other interview analysts when all of their trials are concluded."

I stand there dumbfounded as I'm untied from the post. Behind me is a hallway lined with more cells like mine. I'm thrown into the first one on the left. I don't bother getting up or trying to escape as the door is closed. Instead, my mind starts running.

I didn't murder anyone. I've never murdered anyone, nor have I wanted to murder anyone. I can't die for something I didn't do. I can't die. But I have nothing left. My wife is gone, and people act like she never existed. They're just hiding her. She is real. She's as real as I am.

But what if they're right? No, she's real. She's very real. She was with me through everything. It's impossible for her not to be real. But she's gone now. She's not here to comfort me. She can't hold me or tell me I'll get through this. No one is here to help.

Will I die alone? Will I die with no one to hold, no one who loves me, no one who cares?

If I die, then this will all be over. There won't be any more pain, any more suffering. No, I don't want to do that. I don't . . . I don't want to do that . . .

I just want this gone. Just take it all away.

***

Over the next few days, I watch the other trials. From my cell, I'm able to see some of the room, and what I can't see I can hear because my cell is so close. They all happen the same as mine. No other analyst is able to convince the crowd they're innocent. The crowd is just a mob ready to kill anyone on the stand.

While I sit and watch these trials, my mind doesn't stop running. This time, the question of ending it all is on constant replay.

If I die, then this will all be over. When it's over, I'll be free. And when I'm free . . . but what about the afterlife? What if there is none? What if I'm not free? What if my pain continues? Is there even an afterlife? What if everything just stops when you die? Just nothing. My life was pointless and worthless. No one will remember me.

Should I even wait to be killed? What if I just kill myself now? But how would I do that? No, no, no. Stop this. You don't want to do this. But if you do, it could all stop. But what if it doesn't?

I just want to kill myself and be done with all of this. No, you don't. Yes, I do. No, you don't.

"You'll regret it if you go through with it." I turn over and there's a woman at the door. Her voice is familiar, but I know she was the one against the wall that raised her hand.

I sit up and wipe my face off before asking, "Regret what?"

"Killing yourself."

I stare at her in disbelief. "How do you know that?"

The woman looks down a moment before looking back at me and replying, "Someone told me."

"My wife?" I ask, excited. She's the only one who ever knew.

"No, but it's someone who cares."

"Who?" I ask, feeling destroyed again.

"They . . . they wanted me to tell you my story. Because I've been through the same thing you have."

I turn away from the woman. "No one has been through what I have—no one knows what I've gone through, let alone would they be able to help me."

"I don't believe that."

"My help was getting off this planet. That was what was going to help me. Getting out of the job that started it all and being around people who care about their lives. That's what was going to help."

"I thought the same way you did. I thought leaving what initially caused the problem would solve it. If anything, it made it worse."

"You can't help me."

Out of the corner of my eye, I see the woman sit down next to the door. "I've wanted to kill myself before."

"You . . . really?" I ask.

"I even knew exactly how I would do it. Had it all planned out. It was trying to do it that was the hardest. I was there for almost five hours trying to do it, but I couldn't do it. I was so emotionally distraught, I passed out. Let me tell you, you don't want to go there."

"Why . . . why didn't you do it?" I ask, looking at her.

"I kept thinking about the people that loved me."

"No one loves me." I look away from her.

"God does."

"What?"

"The one who told me to tell you my story. It was God. He loves you."

"But . . . if He does, why don't I feel it? I could feel my wife. She loves me."

"Have you asked?"

"No."

"Then . . . try asking. You can ask him anything, you know."

"How'd you get past us?" A man walks up and lifts the woman off the ground. "No talking to the terrorists."

"Ask him to take it all away," the woman says as she leaves my view.

I pull my knees up to my chest and wrap my arms around them as I rock back and forth. A while after the woman was taken away, my mind starts to run again.

I curl up in the corner of the room and cry, facing away from the door so no one can see me in such a mess.

As I lie here sobbing with nothing else to do, I try it. I just ask that it's taken all away. I whisper it. And to my surprise, I fall asleep without waking up once or having any sort of nightmare.

9

The next morning I wake up with questions, but my mind isn't spiraling. Why did I fall asleep all right? How did I fall asleep? Who is this woman, and why is she helping me?

A guard walks by my door, and I run over to it. "I need to see that woman from yesterday."

"No one gets to visit the prisoners." The guard doesn't stop walking.

"I have to see her. Please?" The guard doesn't reply and continues walking.

I grab my hair and pace back and forth in the room. I need to see her. I need to see her. I pace for so long that I create a path in the ground. I can't stop moving because I need to do something. Hopefully, if I do something, I won't start thinking again, and if I don't start thinking, then I won't spiral. While I pace, I watch the guard walk back and forth in the hallway. A while later, the woman walks up to my door.

I jump to the door the second I see her and start spouting off questions. "Who are you? Why did I sleep so well last night? What in the world is going on?"

"Quiet." She puts her finger over my lips and whispers, "Did you ask him to take it away?"

I nod my head.

"That was God. That wasn't me. And God wants to help you. He doesn't want you to suffer."

"If He doesn't want that, then why did I suffer in the first place?"

"You sinned, and sin can lead to suffering. But the great thing about God is that he can take our suffering and turn it for good."

"How can good come out of suffering? Look at me, nothing good is coming from this ever."

"Without God, I would agree with you. But God is the miracle worker. What we see as suffering, God uses that to grow us and make us better and more than we ever could have been before"

"I don't understand."

"God plans to prosper you and not to harm you, plans to give you hope and a future."

"I don't . . . I don't understand."

"Then ask God for understanding."

"Hey, how'd you get past again?" a guard yells.

"I'll be back tomorrow. Be ready," the woman says just as she's grabbed by the guards.

"Be ready for what?"

She doesn't answer, and I step back from the door. I sit down and process everything that just happened. My mind races, but again, I don't spiral out of control. I just process what I was told and think it through.

By the end of the night, I've gotten nowhere, so I start thinking again, which leads to me spiraling, which causes me to cry myself to sleep for the thousandth time. Just like any other day. I'm broken. I can't be fixed.

10

I WAKE UP TO the crowd back again in the big room as another analyst is put on trial. When the trial starts, the man with the pole says, "This is the last subject. The executions will begin this evening."

This evening! No, no, no. I can't die now. I look out the door and see no sign of the woman. Where is she? I am not dying.

I pace back and forth through the room, even though I feel I shouldn't. My mind starts racing, and it takes everything in me not to let my mind spiral.

As I pace, a group of guards comes up to the door, one of them the bandanna guard from before. "Weren't you the one who didn't have a wife?"

"I have a wife," I say as I continue to pace.

"You really had a wife?" asks another guard.

"Yes! Did you not hear me the first time?"

"Ha-ha. Pay up." The bandanna guard holds out his hands, and the other guards fill his hands with coins.

I stop pacing and ask, "What are you doing?"

"What does it look like, idiot?" the bandanna guard says, turning around and shoving the coins in his pockets. "I put out a bet that you would still believe you had a wife. And I won."

"I do have a wife," I whisper.

"See, he still believes it." The bandanna guard points at me like an animal in a cage. The rest of the guards make cruel jokes and mock me as they leave.

I sit in the corner of the room away from the door so no one can see me and let it all out, again. I pull my knees up to my chest and wrap my arms around them.

I have a wife. I know I have a wife. They just want to see me suffer. But what if they're right? What if I don't have a wife? What if I never had a wife? That can't be true. She was real. I held her and hugged her and kissed her. She was real. She was very real.

***

AFTER WHAT FEELS LIKE an eternity as I'm in the middle of spiraling, the woman walks up to the door and opens it.

I barely hear it through my sobs, only looking up when she touches my shoulder. I slowly look up and wipe my face with my sleeve. "Why are you here?"

"You want out, don't you?"

I shake my head. "Just let me die. I'm a crazy freak who is broken and can't fix himself."

The woman squats down in front of me with her hand still on my shoulder. "You do realize there is only so much you can fix yourself before you need God."

"Would you quit it with God!" I yell. "Look at me. Doesn't look like He's helping me now, does it?"

"Did you ask him for help?"

"Why can't He just do it!"

The woman looks down for a moment, then back up at me. "Just have faith. Even faith the size of a mustard seed is enough."

"Just leave me. Let me die. No one cares anyway."

The woman holds her hand on my shoulder for a moment before standing up and walking toward the door.

"Do you want to be fixed?"

I look up at her and nod.

"Come on," the woman grabs my hand and leads me down the hallway.

"Where are we going?" I ask, escaping the woman's grasp and walking next to her.

"We're getting out of here."

"I thought I was supposed to be executed?"

"This is what God told me to do."

"He told you to do this?"

"Yes. Through here." She opens a set of double doors opposite the hallway we just were in. We enter another hallway and stop at a door in the middle of the hallway. The woman opens the door, and I'm blinded by the light that shines through.

The woman shields her eyes, and we walk through another hallway that leads outside. When my eyes adjust, I'm greeted by a beautiful landscape. Rolling plains and mountains dot the landscape, with lakes and rivers in abundance. It's the most beautiful thing I've ever seen.

The woman guides me over to a tree and grabs a backpack from one of the low-hanging branches. "Take this. It has everything you need. There's another settlement that way." She points toward a mountain opposite from where we stand. "They won't know your past there. You should be able to live out your life. Now go, before they realize you're gone."

The woman starts walking back the way we came.

"Wait," I yell, and she stops and turns around. "You can't leave. I thought you were going to fix me?"

"You don't need me. You need God."

"But you've helped me."

"God helped you—don't be afraid."

"Afraid?" I throw my hands up. "You just told me to walk across to this giant mountain in a place I've never seen before, I have no idea if my wife is real, and you said you'd fix me. You can't just leave me."

The woman exhales and walks up to me. "I don't want to leave you. But I still have work to do here."

"Like what?"

"I have to go tell everyone about to be executed about God."

"I can't do this alone. I need someone with me."

At that, the woman puts her hands on my head and says, "In Jesus' name, I rebuke this fear controlling this man. I ask that he would trust You, God, to be his guide and light unto his path forward. I ask that he would trust You and lean into you for help and guidance and that he would come to know You and have a relationship with You. In Jesus' name, amen."

She drops her hands, and we stare at each other. "He will help you," she says. "Just let Him in."

After a moment, I say, "Why am I getting the feeling that you love me? You act just like my wife. She doesn't care about my brokenness but loves me for who I am while trying to help me through my brokenness."

The woman smiles. "I understand. You don't have to have a wife for someone to love you. I love you, as does God."

"Why do you love me?" I ask.

"Why do you ask?"

"I . . . I didn't think anyone but my wife would because of my brokenness."

"I don't believe you're broken. You're searching, and you're finding your answers."

I grin at her, and she grins back. "You better get going." She pats my shoulder and turns around. "I almost forgot—there's a Bible in your backpack. It's the Word of God. That'll answer your questions."

"Will I ever see you again?" I ask.

"One day," she says with confidence as she walks back through the door.

I turn around and stare in amazement at the landscape in front of me. I have no idea where I'm going. No clue what exactly happened in the past few days. No idea where my wife is. And no clue as to why any of this is even happening. All I know is that this woman loves me, as does God. Hopefully that's enough to get me through to this new settlement.

As I take my first step, I know I should be feeling fear, but I'm not. I almost feel a little excited.

As I take my second step, I smile genuinely for the first time in what feels like forever—not afraid, not scared, and with a purpose to find out more about God, why He helped me, why He cares for me, and why He loves me.

IF YOU ARE LOOKING for healing and would like to start a relationship with Jesus Christ, say the following out loud.

Dear Jesus, I am a sinner. I ask for forgiveness and repent of my sin. I confess that you are the Son of God, the Savior, and that you died on the cross for my sins. I confess that you rose from the grave three days later, defeating death. I ask that you come into my life. I accept you as Lord and Savior of my life. I want to live for you and follow you. Write me in your book of life. In Jesus's name, amen.

If you prayed that prayer and believed in your heart and confessed with your tongue, then welcome to the Kingdom of Heaven. I don't want you to take your journey with God alone. Please reach out to me on social media, my website, and at the number below.

Grace Church: (317) 535-5640

You can also call this number if you or a loved one have struggled with suicide.

I want to connect with you and get you connected with others who will help you navigate your life as a follower of Christ and help grow your faith. Welcome to the Kingdom, brother/sister.

This book is easily the hardest book I've written to date. At the time of writing this, it's over two months before the book will be released, and it may be even harder to let this book go. But I can really thank only one person that this was written in the first place, and that is Jesus Christ. I guarantee you things would be different if you weren't in my life. Thank you for surrounding me with your faithful servants to help me navigate this season of my life. And thank you for showing me one of the lessons from this season. All I can say is thank you, thank you, thank you.

Thank you also to the people who helped make this book a reality, my editors Karen and Pamela. I can't thank you enough for getting this book presentable and readable for those who pick up this story.

And last, but certainly not least, I want to thank all of you who read this story. I pray that this has changed your life or will help you change someone else's life. I write for you to have a positive change in your life, and I pray this book is able to do that and more. I encourage you to share this book with others. Tell them about it, give them your copy, and let others be changed as you hopefully have been.

Thank you also for supporting me in the first stages of my career as an author. You all are the start of something that I believe will be big one day.

AFTER DROPPING OUT OF college to publish his first book Prime Youth: Prisoners of the Masquerade, E.E. hasn't put his pen down. And with too many ideas to count he won't be putting that pen down anytime soon. When he has to force himself to stop writing he does the next best thing, reading. He also enjoys hiking and is actively involved in his home church, ensuring E.E. has a steady stream of inspiration and friends to help him along his journey.

Website: eecooley.com

Instagram: @e.e.cooley

Facebook: E.E. Cooley

Twitter: @EE_Cooley